The Witch's Curse

The Witch's Curse

K.P. KNUPP

ISBN: 979-8-9932255-3-1 (Paperback)

ISBN: 979-8-9932255-2-4 (e-book)

Editing by: Kristen Susienka

Cover design and Tarot Cards by: insta-love graphic design

Illustration by Marta Riva - Into The Forest Illustrations
@marta.intotheforest

intotheforestillustrations.com

 Formatted with Vellum

Also by K.P. Knupp

Snowed In at the Cabin

Alexandra (Alex) Lewis has been biding her time—putting in late nights and early mornings—to become the web designer at Johnson Enterprise. After being passed over (again and again) she makes the rash decision to quit her job. She now has limited time to find a new career or risk having to move back in with her parents.

Desperate to make a living on her art, she needs to find a way back to her creativity and build up her portfolio. Alex impulsively books a secluded getaway at a cabin in the woods. When a wild winter storm comes crashing through faster than initially anticipated, she ends up snowed in with the owner of the cabin, James Edward. The same James who she can't seem to stop bumping into after quitting her job. He seems to be everywhere. From moving into the same building to faking a relationship when her newly ex-boyfriend shows up at the club, they're drawn together.

Snowed in at a cabin in the woods seems fine until the power goes out, and they're left with one bed in front of the fireplace to stay warm. Will the bubble break once they're free from the cabin?

The Witch's Curse

Rachel's curse is nothing new. She's dealt with it her entire life. One day every year filled with bad luck.

But when Caleb, a handsome wizard ,comes to town, things start getting worse than ever before. Spilled coffee is one thing. But when her magic starts backfiring and a seers premonition looms overhead, it's time to dig deeper for a cure.

Rachel and Caleb have one day to unravel the curse, or risk it becoming worse than they could ever imagine.

A Wild Run

We put together this anthology to showcase the very real enigma of human creation. In a world increasingly complacent with AI, we wanted to prove a point: You can give the same prompt over and over to a machine and it will spit out the same, if not largely similar output. Give authors the same prompt... and watch what the human mind can do.

This Mess We Live In

Through the various degrees of life we experience love and pain. To be able to experience it at all is a blessing, but at times it still hurts. While new love can light you up again.

This is for the healing journey. For the fear of the unknown and how diving in can often times be the only answer.

There's brightness on the other side, you just have to keep going.

Fade

Ali doesn't know if she's going crazy, or if what she's feeling is real. There's a presence trying to get her attention, but what happens when she decides to believe.

Contents

For my beautiful son
and all the clumsy people in this world,
your bruises will heal,
embarrassment will fade,
and no one will remember
that awkward thing you did.

Chapter One

For as long as I can remember, every year on Samhain —or Halloween, as the non-witches call it—I've been cursed with an entire day of bad luck. For years this has been problematic when celebrating with my coven. I've suffered some terribly embarrassing moments—everything from a failed, basically poisonous soup for the harvest ceremony to accidentally starting half the woods on fire when I should have made a bonfire. Let's just say given my track record, no one asks for my help anymore, and I'm basically sequestered inside for a whole day as a security measure.

"Rachel Evans! Where do you think you're going?" Becks, my best friend-slash-business-partner-slash-roommate yells as she rounds the corner.

I inherited the house we live in when I turned eighteen. My parents passed away in a tragic accident when I was ten, but no one in the coven has told me specifics beyond that. Just that when I'm old enough I will have to figure it out for myself. Well, I'm twenty now, cursed beyond repair, and have no idea what happened ten years ago. My aunt Viv raised me, but even she has been tight-lipped.

"Oh no." I clutch my messenger bag closer to my body, trying to slink over to the front door. "I'm sorry. I have to. I need coffee, and you have to go open the bookstore!" We bought a bookstore this year in our quaint town of Cyprus, Massachusetts, with a total population of ten thousand humans and witches. Being co-owners we both just fell into our respective roles. I enjoy making potions and baking, when it's not curse day, and Becks loves to dive into the books and mingle with the locals, ever the chatty witch.

Becks holds a fresh container of scones in her hands, ready to load with the rest of the baked goods we sell at the store. I usually help with the baking, but once midnight strikes on Samhain, I'm not really allowed anywhere that danger can follow.

"You can't go without a pumpkin spice latte for one day? You know bad things can happen even at a coffee shop," Becks scolds, her blonde curls swishing over her shoulders as she shakes her head. Her slight smile lets me know she's only half serious.

We found each other in kindergarten and haven't let go since. Her parents expected a lot from her, demanding she practice magic until her fingers ached or hounding her to do something spectacular with her life, but they were also absent. They are two of the coven leaders, and they take their jobs extremely seriously. Every time they would go to meetings when we were younger, Becks would slip out and come to my house. We would stay up late baking and singing songs at the top of our lungs.

Klaus, her black cat, starts weaving between her legs and shooting daggers at me. "Menace," I grumble to him. To Becks I say, "I know. I know. But can you blame me? It's every year. No one knows how to break the curse, and I still need to live my life!" I lower my voice after it cracks, my emotions getting the better of me. "Plus, if I have to watch the store all night while you go to the celebration, I'll need a latte to keep me company." My back hits the door and somehow rattles enough that the lamp on our entryway table falls and shatters all over the floor. I grimace. My shoulders jump to my ears, the sound jarring my senses. "I'll pick up a new lamp while I'm out."

Becks sighs, then waves her hand, and the pieces of the lamp float in the air toward the trash can. They drop in with another crash, making me jump. She was gifted with fire magic and telekinesis, the ability to move things with her mind. As an earth witch, I've always envied that Becks grew into a second element and I didn't.

"Don't bother until this night is over," Becks says as she leans against the wall. "There's no point in breaking a brand new one too."

Klaus jumps onto the couch near the door, looking me up and down until Fred, my black cat, barrels down the hallway toward me, yowling.

"Fred, calm down. I will only be gone for a short time." I glance at Becks as Fred slams into the side of my leg before righting himself. "Becks can bring you to the shop, so you can be with me all night." He purrs in response, rubbing against my legs.

Becks sighs again. "If he bolts to look for you, I'm leaving his ass behind."

Fred whips his head toward her, puffing up.

"I said what I said," Becks says. "You behave or you're living on the streets." She folds her arms across her chest like she means business, but we both know she's a major softy for the idiot and would never leave him behind.

Klaus lets out a meow that has Fred walking toward Becks and sitting at her feet like a good boy. Klaus is older, barely, and loves to boss Fred around. I shrug at Fred and open the door. "See you soon! Thanks for taking Fred."

As I swing the door shut, Becks shouts, "Don't use your magic! You know what it does today!"

Yeah, yeah. Like a witch could go a day without using magic. As if.

My curse is a pain in the ass, but it could be worse. It could backfire every single day rather than one day a year. I shiver. *Ugh that would be horrendous. I better not put that into the universe, or it will probably come true next year.*

I picture the set of grimoires I found tucked away in my aunt's basement a few years ago. They were stacked behind boxes of decorations long forgotten and covered in three inches of dust. I'll go through them tonight too, like usual, and pray the truth behind my "predicament" is hidden in those pages.

Each year I search the witch's library and spend all day looking for a counterspell to cure me of this annual drudgery. When I was younger, Aunt Viv or members of the coven would help, but now it's just me. I don't like burdening others with my little problem, so I have taken it upon myself to continue the search.

It's a cool autumn day, the light breeze perfect for my favorite light blue sweater. Samhain is literally the best day ever. It's too bad I haven't been able to experience it in all its glory. *Yet.* When I was younger, Aunt Viv brought me to a few, but it was short lived when the pull to use magic would create chaos. But I refuse to give up hope. I have a feeling this year might be different.

Curse aside, I still love everything about the holiday—the decorations, the bonfires, the food, the dancing. Even if all of it is too dangerous for me to partake in. One day soon I'll be free from this curse and spend the entire night up into the morning right in the middle of the festival.

I wiggle my fingers at the flowerbed lining the cobblestone sidewalk and watch as the flowers shoot up and explode in reds and oranges until fully bloomed. Our small town is lined with cobblestones that give an old-timey feel. It's cozy here. I admire the full flowers lining the sidewalk.

See, there's no problem with my mag—

A root snakes across my path and wraps around my ankle, effectively taking me out as I roll across the stone. "Ugh! Really! I was just trying to help the flowers grow." I untangle my ankle and sit there watching the root slither back into the dirt.

"Rude."

Chapter Two

I brush myself off and continue into town. I wave to Ms.
Mills, who's out setting up pumpkins along her walkway. Her husband died last year, and they never had children, so everyone makes an effort to check in on her
throughout the week. She loves coming to the shop, so Becks
and I have adopted her as our honorary grandmother.

"Girl, shouldn't you be locked inside?" Ms. Mills squawks
when she sees me. "You better not be baking for the festival."
She props a hand on her hip, her graying hair floating in the
breeze.

I throw my head back, laughing. "I would never dream of
it after the hate mail I received a few years ago. It's just a little
bad luck, nothing serious." I shrug off her worries. She's
invested in helping me cure the curse. Always bringing me
new concoctions to drink. All of them more awful than the
last and no more effective.

She harrumphs, a hint of a smile spreading across her lips
as she picks up another pumpkin from her wheelbarrow and
places it next to the others. She's known me since I was a child.
My coven has known about the curse since I was born. They

just didn't understand the extent of it until I was older and the curse grew more out of control. Every year it gets a little worse, but I keep that to myself.

Legend has it that one of my distant relatives angered a warlock by choosing her soulmate instead of him, so he cursed her future generations. The problem with curses is that they're fickle beasts that choose their own paths if a witch's wording isn't pristine. Thus, generations later, lucky ol' me gets the curse. The mark of the moon on my shoulder signaled to everyone that I had been chosen, and so the coven wrapped a bubble around much of my life.

It's a personal choice to avoid the festival and embarrassing myself every year. Occasionally, sure. But lately I enjoy keeping most of my mess to myself and digging through ancient texts looking for answers. Besides, Becks started dating one of the few men from our coven a few months ago, and being a third wheel doesn't sound exciting. I'm not interested in dating for the fun of it anymore. I've known all the men around my age since I was young, and none of them scream husband material.

Every witch and wizard from our coven has tried their best to reverse the curse, but it's as stubborn as I am.

I'll get it eventually. I hope.

himes ding above the door as I step inside the only coffee shop in town and take a deep breath. I close my eyes, reading the atmosphere. I love the smell of fresh coffee, the excited chatter from everyone enjoying a warm cup of their choice of poison, and the *swoosh* of the milk steamer. Someone behind me clears their throat, and my eyes snap open. "I'm sorry," I mumble and rush over to the ordering line.

The girl behind the register looks up at me, wearing a wide smile, her purple hair piled high on her head. "Good morning! What can I make for you?"

Everything about her puts me at ease. *I needed this, to be out in the world.* "A large pumpkin spice latte, please."

"Perfect! Slide your card on the screen, and you can pick it up on the other side when they call your order." She beams at me again, then moves on to the next person.

I scurry toward the other counter and wait in a corner near the wall, trying not to have any mishaps with other customers. I wish this curse would go away already. I've tried everything. Well, besides eating frog hearts, which Aunt Viv swears by, but

I'm not that desperate yet. *Ugh*. Just thinking about it makes me shiver.

"Large pumpkin spice! Large black coffee!" the worker behind the counter yells.

I snatch my latte off the counter and take a sip. "Aahhh, perfection," I whisper. Now I'm ready to lock myself in the store for the rest of the day.

I whip around, about to skip out of the coffee shop, when I slam into a hard chest. My paper cup smashes into whoever I bumped into, and a splash of scalding liquid soaks through my clothes, burning my skin. "Ow! Hot, hot, hot!"

I try to peel my coffee-stained sweater away from my body in hopes the burning sensation will go away. I look down and notice my skin turning bright red, both from the hot coffee and the heat of embarrassment spreading over my neck and cheeks.

Becks was right. I shouldn't have made a pit stop on the way to the bookshop.

I want to cry. My coffee is gone. My clothes are ruined.

"I'm so sorry!" I hear a guy say. "I didn't see you there. Here, let me help you." The man I slammed into reaches for napkins on the counter. I scan his clothing to see if I burned him too, but he's surprisingly dry.

Stupid curse.

"Unfortunately, you can't, but thanks." I lower my head and steel my nerves to brave a walk home to change, when I feel a light touch on my elbow. I gaze up at him and notice his eyes lingering on my neck. I reach for my necklace and tap the pendant that bears my coven insignia and magical ability. It must have slipped when I was freaking out about my shirt. I quickly tuck it back under my neckline.

He points at a table in the corner. "Come over here and let me at least *try* to help you. I promise I don't bite." His smile disarms me.

I love any chance to make my life even messier than it already is, so of course I follow him across the room. I feel disgusting. The sugary concoction that was my latte is making my skin stiff with stickiness. With every step, I smell the autumnal spices that should be on my taste buds.

The guy pulls out a chair facing away from the crowd and motions for me to sit.

I slide into the seat, my eyebrows drawn together, I'm skeptical about how he plans to help me. After everything that has already happened today, I can't be mean to a random stranger who is trying to do a good deed. I'm not sure what that says about me, but here goes nothing. "So, uh . . . what's your plan?" My voice cracks from my almost-emotional event. I could kick myself.

His green eyes sparkle in the light, and his cream-colored sweater complements his dirty blond hair. He's looking at me like he wants to do more than help me clean up spilled coffee. But I'm a walking disaster, so there's no way I can entertain any romantic interest, especially not on Samhain.

I need to get out of here.

"Why don't you tell me what you're most excited to celebrate tonight?" he asks.

"I—wait. What did you say?"

He starts swirling his hands in small circles above the table, then wiggles his fingers at me. I feel the light brush of water then a warm breeze. I glance around, but no one is looking in our direction. "You're a wizard?" I say, wide-eyed. "With water *and* air magic?"

I brush my hands over my favorite blue sweater. It's fully clean, dry, and beautiful again.

He chuckles. "I'm happy I could help. I noticed your pendant, which made this easier." He points at my shirt. "Otherwise I would've used these useless napkins."

"Yeah, magic is always better." I sigh, sitting back in my seat. "Too bad you don't have coffee magic."

"What's your order? It smelled like spices." He gets up and pulls out his wallet.

"Oh no. It's okay. I should probably get going. I'm not really . . ." I bite my lip. *How do I explain what my problem is?* "I will probably spill it again." I say simply, choosing not to dive into it.

He waves me off. "Well it's a good thing that I'm here to clean up. You have two options. You tell me what you want, or I pick something random off the menu."

My nose scrunches involuntarily. "Okay, okay. Pumpkin spice latte, please."

He smiles, pleased, and takes off to the counter again.

While I wait for him to return, I pull out my phone.

> Rachel: Oh my goddess! You'll never guess what happened to me!

> Becks: You spilled coffee everywhere?

> Rachel: No…Well yes, but I met a wizard! He cleaned everything…with magic…AND he's getting us more coffee!

> Rachel: I think I'm in love

> Becks: Not on this day you're not! You already know all the wizards in town. Is the curse getting to your brain?

> Becks: Are you trying to get it to ruin your life permanently?!

> Rachel: He's new I think, not from here that I've ever seen. Ugh. It's not that bad. It's just a bit of bad luck. It's never been malicious. Just annoying.

> Becks: What about that time…

> Rachel: Do not bring up the tray of muffins. I swear!

> Becks: Okay. Okay. Don't fall too hard, muffin woman. We have a store to run.

> Becks: And by "we" I mean you….I have a party to go to!

> Rachel: Haha yeah. I'll be there soon!

I slide my phone back into my pocket as the wizard returns to the table holding my delicious latte and whatever he ordered. "Thank you!" I take the cup and almost melt. "Mmm. I'm Rachel, by the way." I take a sip and watch him over the rim of my cup.

"Caleb." He slides into the chair across from me and sets his paper cup on the table. His eyes never leave my face.

I squirm under his intense stare. "Well, Caleb. I need to get to my store, but I really appreciate the new coffee." I push my chair back to stand, and he does the same. His muscular build tugs against his cream sweater. I think I'm falling faster the more I look at him.

I need to get to the store!

"It's no problem at all. Really." He runs a hand through his dirty blond hair. "I guess I'll continue wandering the town."

I was right. He's not from around here.

I keep a tight grip on my new coffee, unwilling to let it

splatter on the floor again, or on my clothing. "There's a lot of fun events tonight. I'm sure you'll enjoy them." I force my smile to stay small and turn to go.

"I'll walk out with you," Caleb says. "Maybe we could meet up later for the celebration." He rushes forward and opens the door for me.

This is the moment I dread. "Sorry, but I don't go to the celebration." I bite my cheek and wait for the inevitable response.

"Okay. Where's your store? Maybe I can bring you a new latte in a few hours. I mean, if you'd like that?" His green eyes dart to the street as he quickly takes a drink. He slides his other hand into his pocket as his eyes find mine again. The energy coming off him takes my breath away. But no. I *cannot* catch feelings on Samhain.

But I also can't contain the smile stretching across my face as we head in the direction of the shop. "I would love that, actually. It's down the block, on the corner. The Bookish Baker."

He stops short, his eyebrows shooting up his forehead. "*You* are *the* bookish baker?" We don't ship out orders, so the only way someone would know about our shop is if they visited our tiny town. Which happens. We get tourists, but Cyprus isn't a huge travel destination. Everyone would rather go to Salem, especially near Halloween.

"Well, I'm half of it. It's me and Becks, my best friend. You've heard of us?" The sidewalk is starting to congest with people coming out for the celebration and trick-or-treating. I point toward the shop and walk faster. Being trampled isn't on my daily horoscope.

Caleb weaves between people until he's beside me again. "My grandparents have talked about it, so it was on my list of places to see while I'm here. Do you mind if I check it out before everything gets wild? I'll still come back later with coffee. Promise."

Maybe I'm feeling the loneliness of my curse day, or his charm is working overtime on me, but either way, I lead him to the shop. "I don't mind. We like to think our shop is a home away from home for people. Witches especially." I look at him, our eyes locking once more. His smile grows.

"That's amazing," he says as he helps me navigate through the mass of people. It's like everyone is starting their night now, or we have more out-of-towners than usual.

I peel my eyes away from him when we reach the corner. "Well, here it is!"

I try to take in the view from a new person's perspective. The old brick exterior is a light pink. The sign on the door reads *The Bookish Baker*, and mugs and scones float around the text. It's pretty and welcoming. And will always have a piece of my heart.

Caleb reaches for the door and holds it open for me.

The smell of freshly baked muffins and scones wafts around us as we enter. Books line the walls, and five tables and a couch dominate the middle. Plants fill in empty space around the books and form each table's centerpiece. Behind our front desk, various herbs and flowers hang upside-down to dry.

The back room holds vials of herb/oil mixtures of intent —spell ingredients for witches in need. The ingredients aren't advertised to humans, but if witches visit, there are signs around the room that only they would notice. Symbols hidden on bookshelves, walls, and teacups. Becks and I have a large garden at our house where we pull the ingredients from. Some we dry at home, others here, depending on the day and if we need to work.

The bells chime as we enter. Two tables have people reading at them, while the rest of the store is quiet. Witches are outside preparing for the celebration and the humans are dressing up for their night of trick-or-treating.

"I'll be right there!" Becks yells from the back room.

Caleb looks around, slowly turning to take in every inch. He wanders to our wall of authors to the right of the register. Every writer who has visited or held signings here has autographed the wall. But it's getting so full that we're going to have choose another wall for them to sign soon.

"Wow. You have quite a few big names here," he whispers, still reading.

"You're a reader?" I take in his wild wind-tossed hair as he traces the names with his finger. It reminds me of meadow grass, unkempt but still beautiful. In jeans and a sweater, he's not overly dressed for the celebration, but he's not from around here so maybe he doesn't realize this small town goes a bit overboard with tradition.

Everyone wears gowns or suits, but the vast majority ends up barefoot and shirtless by the end of the night. The coven takes over after darkness settles, and a large section of the woods is set up for gathering. Tables are lined with food or games where magic is the biggest strategy, and near the bonfire, dancers of all levels of grace and craze twirl in the moonlight well into the morning hours.

Becks's boots clack on the wooden floor as she pushes through the back door. "Good. You're back! Did anything else happen with the curse—" She squeaks, taking in the daggers I'm shooting at her. I tilt my head toward Caleb. "The coffee," Becks says. "I mean the coffee. Did anything else happen with the coffee?"

Great save. I could throttle her sometimes. "Nope. Everything was fine. Totally normal day."

Caleb swivels, taking in Becks with her purple-and-orange-patched dress and black boots before smiling and holding out his hand. "I'm Caleb. You must be Becks, the other owner."

Becks shakes Caleb's hand slowly. "Yeah, how did you know that?" She side-eyes me. "Rachel, what have you been telling this man? I swear . . ."

"Nothing! I just told him about our amazing store, but he already knew about it. I walked him here so he could check it out before he tours the town." I'm sweating. I feel like a teenager again being interrogated by Aunt Viv for staying out late.

"Right." She draws out the word like she doesn't believe me. Which is fair. I mean, nothing else happened—yet. But the day is young.

Caleb's head bounces between us like a Ping-Pong ball. "Your store is awesome. I've heard nothing but good things." He studies the herbs drying behind the desk. "What did you mean earlier about a curse? Are you in trouble?"

I groan. Damn wizards always wanting to fix us. "Nothing. It's really fine."

Becks shoots me a glare. "It's fine?" She taps her boot and crosses her arms.

Fred takes this moment to sprint at me from the back room before launching himself at my chest. It's like a slow-motion film: I try to catch him with one hand at the same time his paws kick out to cling to me, and the new coffee speeds to the floor. The lid breaks free and splatters all over my pants. I hang my head while Fred rubs my chin, purring like he's a good boy for tossing my second coffee everywhere.

Becks stares at us. "I told you coffee wasn't a good idea."

"Is your magic allergic to pumpkin spice? That's the second cup that's attacked you." Caleb peeks at the customers, who seem absorbed in their books. He moves his hands, cleaning the coffee off my clothing and leaving me nice and dry again.

"Thanks." I rub the fur between Fred's ears as he purrs

louder, making biscuits on my sweater. "I'm not sure what's happening with the coffee."

Becks raises her eyebrows at me. "I do."

I frown.

"So, what is a wizard doing in our small town on Samhain?" Becks says, sizing Caleb up. "Don't you have your own festival to attend?" She's not wrong. Most covens stay together during celebrations. Though it's not unheard of for the younger generation to travel, they usually go with friends. Caleb seems on his own.

"Becks!" I scold, but she shrugs and waves her hand at Caleb.

He grins and stares at the floor. "It's a little complicated."

Strange.

Fred jumps from my arms as I ask, "Complicated how?" Becks walks over to me and bumps her shoulder against mine.

Caleb's eyes close like he regrets being asked about why he's here. "My grandfather is a seer."

I suck in a breath as I look at Becks, full panic flashing in her eyes. Seers are rare witches. There's a handful in the world at any given time. Most like to stay hidden, so they aren't used for their visions.

My head whips to Caleb. "*Annddd?* What exactly did he see? Something about us?"

Seers don't like interfering with their visions, so the fact that Caleb was presumably sent here means it's something big.

Caleb's eyes darken. "Honestly, I don't have a clue."

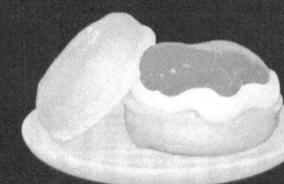

The Bookish Baker

Bookish Baker

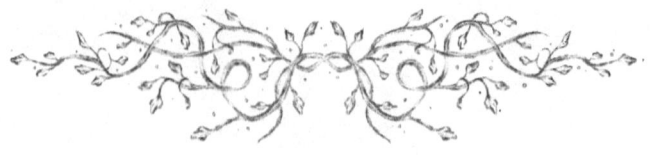

Chapter Four

Caleb grimaces. "He didn't give me details, just a vague command that I would be needed on Samhain at The Bookish Baker. It didn't really feel like a suggestion coming from him, so I jumped in my car and drove here." He shrugs like he's given us a rational response. "So, if either of you have any idea why I'm needed, please enlighten me."

Becks kicks her leg out at me.

"Ouch. Could you not?" I hiss.

"Well, maybe it's for the you-know-what?" She wiggles her eyebrows at me, throwing her head toward Caleb. She's quick to share my secrets, considering we've been told our entire lives that we are not to tell other covens about the curse. Probably based on the fact that no one knows which coven it originated from, and cursing other witches is frowned upon.

I roll my eyes at her wild decision to tell a stranger my business. "Or maybe it's for your demon cat!" I fire back at her.

Becks scoffs. "Hey! Rude. Klaus isn't a demon. He just prefers to be the boss of the house. In a slightly aggressive way." She grimaces at her last line, like she doesn't believe her lies either.

Caleb clears his throat, and we both pivot our attention toward him. "I'm wondering if the reason is this curse you accidently mentioned, but I don't want to push you." He pauses. "I can go for a coffee run again, if you want time to think about it."

"I'm good," Becks says at the same time that I say, "Yes!"

I glower at her. "She means yes. Two of the same will be great, thanks!" I push him toward the door. "See you soon."

He laughs but takes the hint, then walks out the door and saunters back down the street.

I dart my eyes from Becks to the customers and twitch my fingers. Becks spins her hands around each other to summon a sound-proof bubble. The second it's up I ask, "What are you thinking? The coven said we aren't allowed to involve other witches."

Becks sighs. "Rachel, it's been twenty years. I don't think our coven has the solution, so can they really object to asking someone else?" She places a hand on my shoulder. "Perhaps the grandson of a seer holds the key to all of your secrets."

I plop onto the couch, and Becks slides in next to me. "But what if nothing changes?"

She runs her fingers through my hair. We've always been more like sisters than friends. "What if you take a chance on yourself and it changes *everything*?" Tears fill my eyes and I hug her as tight as possible before making her laugh and gasp for air.

"Okay, okay. I love you too. Let me go."

"Oh, stop it, Becks. You love it." I fall backward and close my eyes. "I hope I can finally drink this pumpkin spice latte, or I'm going to really cry."

She flicks my nose. "You're obsessed. Why did you have him get two? You know I hate that shit."

I peek at her, smirking. "I know. It's also for me. In case mine spills for a third time."

"You're insufferable." She stands from the couch and releases the silencing spell.

As the shop's quiet fills our ears again, our two tables of customers pack up their things and wave.

"Have a great night!" We both say at the same time.

"Hey, before you leave," I say to Becks, "can you light all the pumpkins in the window? I want it to look festive for when the little kids come to get candy." I jump up on the counter and swing to the other side to get the giant bowl and endless candy we've been stocking up on.

"You could just light them individually like a human you know? Since your magic doesn't work." Becks says as she snaps her fingers and a flame appears on one wick. She wiggles the rest of her fingers and the fire spreads to the others and then to the pumpkins. Small and controlled flames dance all around the shop.

"Right. Why would I bother when you have fire magic? Even when my magic is working correctly, it still takes me twice as long to conjure one little fire."

Becks brushes imaginary dirt off her shoulder. "You're right. My magic is way cooler than yours." She laughs and dodges the candy I throw at her. "Hey now! That's for the children." She flicks her hand, and the candy on the floor flies back into the bowl.

"Showoff. You just wait until tomorrow. This earth witch is going to be the biggest pain in the ass you've ever had." I put my hand on my hip.

She feigns defeat. "Yeah, I remember last year. The day after, you strung me in your favorite tree and covered me in flowers head to toe while you went on a stroll through town *and forgot about me*!"

Like she could ever let me forget. I've been hearing about

it every month since. "You could've gotten down. You have fire magic, *remember*?" I gesture to the lit pumpkins.

"And hurt your precious tree and plants? I think not. I'd probably end up being the next one cursed by Mother Nature." Becks shivers. "No thank you."

"Yeah, you're probably right." I move a small table near the front door and place the candy bowl in the center. I love seeing all the costumes the kids come in wearing. Everyone's always so excited too. It makes me feel almost normal.

"I'm going to head out," says Becks. "Will you be okay with your new warlock?" She picks up her bag and heads to the door.

"He's not mine. But yes, I'm still a witch. I'll be fine."

Becks points at me. "Your magic is on the fritz today, remember?"

I throw my hands up and flowers rain down on us. "I can still do things. They just don't always stay where I want them to after." I shrug as half the flowers stick to my sweater and pants like glue. "Well, that was dumb."

Becks laughs then leaves, winding down the street toward the pre-festival gathering.

As soon as she's gone, I get to work cleaning the shop the hard way. Without magic.

Chapter Five

I dim the lights and press Play on the spooky playlist I have set for the trick-or-treaters. I can't lock up until they're done with their fun. Plus, I love their energy and costumes, so I might as well entertain myself. This really is the best day of the year even if *my* day is a little whacky.

I'm stuffing my grimoires under the checkout desk when the overhead bell dings. "Happy Halloween!" I yell before I face my first visitor. My smile breaks even further at the man with a mop of blond hair, a cream shirt, and jeans filling the doorway. "Oops, you're not a candy monster."

Caleb chuckles, shaking his head. "What on earth is a candy monster?" He comes to the desk and sets down both coffees, pulling a third one for himself out of the holder. He glances around, then points to the second coffee. "Where's Becks?"

"She had to run to the celebration. I'll drink it." I nod toward the table with the candy bowl. "The candy monsters will be here soon, if you dare to find out." I hop up to sit on the counter and take a cup of magic to my lips. *Aaahhh. I love this.*

Caleb lifts himself onto the counter next to me. "I never turn down a dare." He nudges me, and I dip my head to hide the heat creeping up my cheeks.

Screams and squeals of laughter sound a second later. I give him a smirk before the front door bangs open. A cop, a Dalmatian, a superhero, and a witch run inside screaming, "Trick or treat!" The trick-or-treaters are mostly human or half human children as the witches tend to spend all day setting up games, puzzles, and treats for our own celebration that lasts all night. There are games for small witches and warlocks to try out their magic or their everyday skills. Bobbing for apples, hitting an arrow on the target, creating simple potions, and so much more. It's a day of discovery and coming together.

I jump off the counter and run to their open bags. "Happy Halloween! You all look amazing!" I toss handfuls of candy in each bag.

"Thank you!" they say, watching the candy drop in awe before running back out the building.

I retrieve my coffee and take another sip, careful not to make sudden movements. "You think you can handle that every couple of minutes for the next hour? Or will you bail to hang out with the big kids?" I joke.

Caleb watches me with an intensity that excites me as much as it unsettles me. It sends chills through my body. The hair on the back of my neck stands with a tingle. If I didn't know better, I would think he was casting a spell on me. "No. I like where I am." He bops the end of my nose with a finger before sliding to stand next to me. "But I get to give candy to the next round of kids."

The bells chime as if on a magical ringer. I laugh and wave him to the table of candy.

"Trick or treat!" Parents wave and laugh from the sidewalk as they watch the kids and talk to each other.

"Alright, gather close. We've got a neat trick for *you*." Caleb grabs two big scoops of candy and tosses them in the air. The kids watch as the pieces slowly float to each open bag.

"Wow!" one says.

"That's amazing!" says another.

"Thank you!" They all squeal and run out the door, chattering about the magician in the bookshop.

"Using air magic is cheating," I tell him. "They're going to demand you're here every year now." The light in his eyes dances as he places a hand on either side of me, taking in every tiny piece of my face.

"What's so bad about that?"

I gasp. *I don't know. What* is *wrong with that? Nothing, that's what—except for the curse.* He reaches behind me for his coffee, leaning even closer to my body. He's a hair away from me now. He takes a drink, never dropping his eyes from my face. I want to get lost in the swirl of his irises.

"I—uh. Nothing?" I shrug, immediately feeling like an idiot.

He looks down and stops. "Those flowers weren't there earlier." He tries to pluck one off the hem of my shirt, but it doesn't budge. "What happened?"

"Uh."

The door chimes again, saving me. Caleb goes to the bowl. The door doesn't stop opening after that. A constant stream of kids barrages us for an hour, and the more kids pile in, the more I hope that Caleb forgets his question entirely.

Chapter Six

W hen the last child leaves, I flip the lock and turn off the front lights. "That's it for the kiddos. The festival is officially starting if you want to head to that." I turn, but when I lift my eyes, Caleb's are locked on me and I can't pull myself away.

"And what are you going to do? Want to come show me all the best spots?" Caleb inches closer, never dropping his gaze.

I bite my lip, wanting to sink into the ground and hide. "I can't."

"Why not?" He's a foot in front of me now, and I have to tip my head back to keep my eyes on him.

"Becks told you. I'm . . . cursed." I wait, expecting him to freak out. Yell. Turn me in to the witch's council, who will lock me up to ensure the curse never spreads. All of the things the members of my coven warned me about if I dared to seek help outside of our community.

Caleb runs his hand down my arm to the tips of my fingers and laces his through mine, holding strong. I don't resist. Inside, my body sings. He walks me to a table, and lets go of my hand, so he can pull out a chair for me, then pulls one out for himself. "Cursed with what, exactly?"

I scrunch my face in confusion. "Wait. You're not afraid?"

"No. I told you. I was sent here with a purpose." He interlaces our hands again on top of the table. "I'm not the type of man who runs from a problem."

"What was that purpose again? You were extremely vague on details."

He lets out a whistle. "It's going to sound crazy."

I raise my eyebrows. "I just said I'm cursed, and you think *you're* crazy?"

He laughs, and I relax at the sound. "Okay. You're right. My grandfather is a seer, as you know." I nod. "Seers' visions aren't always fully reliable, but . . ."

"Oh my goddess, spit it out already!" I throw my hands in the air, and flowers explode around us. Caleb glances up and a breeze catches the scattered plants, then places them neatly on the tabletop.

"He told me he saw me at a little bookstore called The Bookish Baker, after closing time, and that there was a challenge we would need to overcome to reach my ultimate fate." He drums his fingers on the table. "'*The path to freedom relies on uniting the heart.*'"

"'*We*'?" I fling my hand between us rapidly. "He *saw* me? And what kind of riddle is that?"

"Not exactly. Seer visions aren't like watching movies in your head. The pictures are foggy and vague. Grandpa could describe small things, but ultimately, I had to come here if I wanted to fill in the details. I'm not sure about the riddle yet, but he insisted it would be important."

He looks so calm, waiting for my reaction. Meanwhile, I'm spiraling inside. "Did you know it was me when we met at the coffee shop?"

"No," he says. "At that point I planned to wander the

streets for hours, if I could even figure it out at all." His lips lift into the faintest smile. "I guess I was just lucky."

I groan and drop my head on the table.

"What did I say?" he asks.

"Luck," I whisper.

"I don't get it. Do you not believe in it or something?"

I lift my head and drag my eyes to his face. "I'm cursed with *bad luck* every year on Samhain. *Forever.* Or that's what we've guessed it is based on what happens."

He sits there staring at me and blinking. *Is he frozen? Aww, hell. My luck got him.* I snap my fingers in his face, and he recoils. "Sorry," he says, shaking his head. "I was . . . thinking. Are you sure that's what it is?"

"I'm sure." I lift my hand toward the small lavender plant growing in a mason jar on our front desk. It shoots up, flowering.

"That looks normal," Caleb says.

"Wait." We watch as the plant stops sprouting flowers. The jar jiggles before the plant's roots jut out, making the container explode. Glass flies in all directions, dirt hits the desk and floor, and the roots snake toward me.

"Hmm. Interesting." Caleb reaches for the roots.

"'Interesting'!" I look from him to the plant. "What part of that is *interesting*?"

Fred runs over and grabs the roots between his teeth then tears off to the back room, his fur puffy. He growls at the plant as dirt flies everywhere.

"Isn't that toxic for cats?" Caleb asks.

"He's fine. Fred is a familiar, he's smart enough not to eat it. He's just also dumb enough to think it's chasing him." I sigh and go to get the broom, but pause when a familiar breeze hits my face. I face Caleb and watch as he uses his air magic to clean up Fred's mess. Dirt swoops together and lifts into the air, floating all the way to the trash behind the counter. When the last speck drops neatly into the bin, he gifts me a small smile.

"Our luck is what we make of it. Unfortunate things happen every day. You may have a bit more on this day, but that's no reason to stop living your life. It's Samhain! Don't you crave connection with nature? You're an earth witch, after all."

I consider his words, feeling the energy pulsing and pulling me toward the earth. My body physically aches to be in contact with nature. "Yes," I whisper.

His air magic whips my hair off my shoulders then rushes to the front windows and blows out every candle. The room sinks into darkness. "Let's go then. The night is young."

I squint to the stack of grimoires I have to go through. A light in the back room buzzes, giving me enough light to see, but barely. "I need to search for answers."

He follows my gaze. "Do you do that every year?" When I shrug, he continues, "I think the best opportunity is for us to try something new. We will come back once we've done some *living* and go through those." He holds his hand out to me, and I reach forward to take it. Maybe he's onto something. Or I'll just be stuck like this for another year. What's the difference?

When our fingers graze a spark jolts my hand, and I jump back. "What was that?" I stare at my hand in wonder. It didn't hurt, just a bright burst of light. There one second and gone the next.

Caleb whistles. "That looked like light magic. It hasn't been seen in centuries."

I laugh. "I don't have light magic. I've only ever had earth magic." I wiggle my fingers, but nothing happens.

"You've also only ever been cursed." He's got me there. "I think we are going to discover new things tonight, but only if we get out of this adorable bookstore." He takes his hand in mine again. Nothing happens, and I'm kind of disappointed as I watch our hands . . . waiting.

Caleb pulls me out the door then pauses so I can lock it. I stop in front of our building, admiring the flowers surrounding the entrance. They're in full bloom, taking in the night air, and calling to me. I brush my fingers against the soft petals of a sunflower, sensing its energy flowing down my arm toward my heart and warming me from the inside. The cool air makes me glad I chose my blue sweater tonight. Unlike Becks, I don't have fire magic to keep me warm.

I slide my sandals off, placing them by the door so I can get them later. Tonight, I need to embrace the earth. Even in cold weather, an earth witch needs to feel the dirt and magical energy at her feet. This is the best time for me to ground myself, letting energy flow through me with every step. The flow of energy up through my feet keeps them at a comfortable temperature, but it doesn't stop the cold air from billowing my hair or clouding my breath.

Caleb waits. "Ready to go into the heart of Samhain?"

"Almost," I tell him. I move out from under the flowery arch and smile as mist kisses my face. I close my eyes and angle my face to the sky. "I needed this."

"I know," he says.

"How?" I lower my chin and lock eyes with Caleb.

He sighs. "A feeling. Are you ready?"

The fuck? "'*A feeling*'? Explain." I'm about two seconds away from tapping my bare foot on this cobblestone walkway causing the ground beneath us to rumble.

He chews his lip. "I can't. It's just a feeling. Like the light when we touched. Every time I'm around you, I get feelings about . . . well . . . you." He watches for a reaction, but I keep my face neutral. "What you need, what you want. It's like an instinct. I don't even think about it before I'm acting."

"This sounds an awful lot like—"

"I know," he says.

"That's . . . crazy." My head is spinning. I feel like I'm going to pass out. "You don't think that's your 'ultimate fate', do you?"

"I guess we will find out." Caleb links his arm through mine and starts walking, diverting my panic. "I think you need a nice cider and some music."

He's right. *Why is he always right?* We walk in a comfortable silence that makes me wonder how we got to this point. It feels as if I've known him my whole life, instead of half a day. I can't explain it.

I peek over at him. He looks so serene, like he belongs in my tiny town. As if he grew up walking these streets every day.

The mist enriches all of the earthy scents. My skin tingles with the energy flowing through me. The more I walk, the more alive I feel. The veil is thinner today, making the magic flow stronger and the ghosts easier to speak to—if a witch wants that kind of connection. Sometimes the ghosts wander freely and seem to enjoy the festivities with their kin.

Caleb nudges my shoulder. "What are you thinking about?"

"That when I'm a ghost, I'll visit on Samhain every year."

He laughs, and the sound wraps around my soul like a warm blanket.

The opening to the park looms in front of us. An array of plants and flowers overflow along the archway, and tiny balls of witch flame float overhead like string lights, and little animals made of water magic run and fly through the grass. A group of children chases them while adults chat nearby, smiling in endless joy. Trays of food and drinks float around, spelled to spin and circle the park so partygoers can grab them at will.

I've missed this. Why did I start hiding away from it all? I inhale the rich earthy aroma surrounding me, because the older one gets the stronger the pull to use magic on Samhain gets. And I've seen too many times what happens when I use magic on this day, let's just hope I can resist the urges.

We cross under the archway and crash into a wave of power, a side effect of having so many magical beings in one location.

"Oh no," I say. I forgot about this part.

Roots from surrounding plants surge for me. I try to leap out of the way, so they can't wrap around my legs, but one latches on and pulls. Power calls to power, which is a problem when my power acts like a fool on this day.

The plant starts pulling me toward its rooted home. My body tips as I careen toward the ground. I reach out to brace for impact, but Caleb wraps an arm around my middle, catching me.

"I've got you." He uses his magic to unwind the plant and send it scurrying back to its home.

"This is why I don't come anymore," I say as I dust off my legs. "I can't do this. I should've stayed in the bookshop with my grimoires."

Caleb grips my hand. "Hold on, Rachel."

I shake my head. "No. It's only going to get worse." I want to crawl inside myself. Go to my safe space and be alone.

He tips my chin up so our eyes meet, and I swear more lights explode inside his gaze. "I'm here. I'll take care of you." He slides his fingers through my hair, hooking some strands behind my ear. My heart skips. "You don't need to be alone anymore. We can face it together."

He leans in close to me, and I swear he's going to kiss me.

"Rachel! I can't believe you came!" Becks runs over to us, breaking the moment. Caleb steps back and slides his hands in his pockets.

Disappointment washes over me. *What is wrong with me? We just met.*

I face my friend and plaster the biggest grin I can manage on my face. "You can blame Golden Boy." I crane my neck to see behind her. "Where's the group you were meeting here?"

She waves a hand. "Eh. I left them when I saw you." She pulls me farther into the festival. "I'm so excited you're here! It's been years since you came. What should we do first?" Becks's excitement is contagious, and soon my doom and gloom has washed away like a bad dream.

I glance at Caleb. "What did you come to see?"

The way his eyes rake over my body then back to my face has my cheeks blazing. *Oh goddess.* He diverts his gaze and scans our surroundings. "Let's start at the apple-bobbing station and work our way around."

"Yes! I'm going to beat both of your times." Becks flits off and we follow behind.

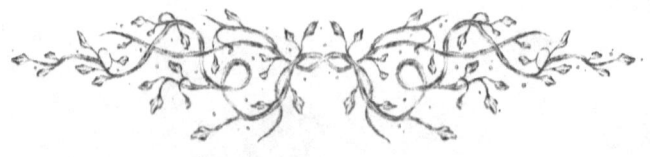

Chapter Seven

Becks slams her face into the freezing water, steam wafting off her skin.

"Cheater!" I shout. "You can't use your fire magic to warm yourself. You need to have the full experience." I nudge her shoulder.

She whips her head up, laughing, an apple snatched between her teeth. She bites off the chunk between her teeth and whirls toward me. "Ah, Rach. Don't be jealous. I'll warm your little cheeks after you're done." She tries to grab me, but I swat her hands away, and we both end up in a fit of giggles.

"Alright. I'm next!" Caleb hovers above the apple bucket, scanning the water for the perfect victim.

"Let's go, Wizard!" Becks yells.

I shush her and hide another giggle behind my hand.

Caleb dives in for half a second before he's back up again with an apple.

Becks gapes at him. "There's no way. Wait." She turns to me and points a finger at Caleb. "Didn't you say he's a water wielder? That's bullshit!"

I double over, clutching my stomach. I can hardly breathe I'm laughing so much.

Caleb pulls his apple free and shrugs. "You used magic first. I figured it was fair game."

"Aarrrggg!" Becks lunges in a sneak-attack tackle that is not very sneaky. On instinct, I reach for my magic and demand that the grass rises up and locks her legs in place. We've played this game since we were ten, so it's second nature at this point. The grass shoots up, snaking around her ankles and up her legs. She shrieks. "You stay out of it, Rachel. Let me get him." Her scream morphs into a cackle.

What a lunatic. "No chance!"

"Uh, what is happening?" Caleb asks, then turns toward the apple bucket.

Becks and I take in the bucket. "Shit," I say. The apples have grown three times their original size.

Becks's eyes are saucers. "Untie me. Quick. We have to run." She flaps her hands at the grass gluing her to the ground.

"You're so dramatic. Why do we need to run?" I ask and release her.

"Because it's fun." If it's possible, her eyes get wider as she locks onto something over my shoulder and starts to jog in place. "And Ms. Mills just saw that you ruined her apples."

She bolts.

I check that Ms. Mills is watching, and see her eyes narrow at us as she walks in our direction. "Shit. Let's go!" I snatch Caleb's hand and dart after Becks. We are all cackling like hyenas by the time we reach the tree line.

Becks falls to the ground, holding her stomach, and I plop down next to her. "Can't. Breathe."

She taps my shoulder then her throat as she open-mouth breathes heavily.

I roll onto my side, away from her. "Stop. Ouch! My side . . . hurts."

"Alright. You two are a mess," Caleb says as a *swish* of air enters my mouth, fills my lungs, and calms my heartrate.

I sit up and fling my head to Becks, whose mouth is hanging open in shock. "What the hell! That's amazing!"

Caleb quirks a brow. "You haven't seen an air magic user?"

"I have, but they've never helped with anything before." Becks jumps to her feet.

I glide my fingers through the grass, letting the waves of energy caress my magic.

Becks holds her hand out to me. "Okay, earth witch. Let's go back. The moon is going to rise soon, then the veil will be the thinnest." She sends me a look as I let her pull me to a stand. "You know what that means."

I brush the grass from my pants. "The ghosts?"

"Yep."

Another reason I stopped coming to the festival. The afterlife can feel my curse, so they are naturally drawn to me. To fix the wrongs of witches. The problem is that all of the ones who came to me over the years didn't have a clue about what happened to my family. When I stayed at the shop, I would just salt the windows so they would leave me alone. But I can't do that here.

"What's happening? What's wrong with the ghosts?" Caleb asks.

"They're drawn to me, so there will most likely be someone trying to connect when the moon rises," I say, unsure if I should just leave now to avoid them. It's not that they just want to talk to me, which they do, but they also don't take no for an answer. Once they have a taste of the curse, they latch on pestering me with questions and useless ideas to try and fix it. Trust me. I listened to a few different ones a couple years in a row and found out the hard way how utterly useless it was.

Caleb studies Becks and me, then his eyes shift to the sky.

"Alright, we have about half an hour to run through all the food carts, eat as much as possible, and go back to the bookshop to research."

"Let's do it!" Becks cheers before taking off in a sprint to the food, not bothering to wait for us.

Typical. "She's obsessed with the food carts on Samhain," I explain.

We start running again. I hear Caleb's footsteps pounding behind me, then catch up to me. He keeps his pace steady with mine.

We stop at the pumpkin cookie stand first and order a dozen so we can take some back with us for the night. We each scarf down a cookie before moving to the apple cider stand. "Three large ciders, please!" I order, digging money out of my bag, but Caleb beats me to it by sending cash to the owner with his air magic.

"Hey, I said I was getting this one," I scold him.

He bops my nose. "And I told you there's no way I'm letting you pay for a thing." He brings his face an inch from mine. "You'll learn to enjoy it."

Becks coughs, and Caleb pulls back with that infuriating smirk on his face. My body is tingling from his closeness. I hate that I want to rush into his arms.

I plant my feet so my body doesn't betray me.

Becks is watching me closely, waiting.

"What?" I ask her.

"Nothing. That was just *very* interesting, is all." She goes to the counter to collect our drinks.

We hit up the caramel apple stand and grab a pumpkin loaf before Caleb and I wave to Becks and make our way back to the bookstore.

"Have fun, you two," Becks calls. "But not too much fun."

My face is on fire with embarrassment. "I have no idea why she said that."

"I do." Caleb says.

Chapter Eight

I unlock the shop door and turn on the lights. Becks and I opted for a warm glow since we aren't open after dark most days. It's enough to read with, but not a harsh glare that makes you dizzy. I grab the grimoires and set them on the large table in the middle of the store for a cozier reading experience.

Caleb whistles. "These are some dark choices. *The Grim Dealings of a Dark Wizard*, *The Afterlife UnEarthed*, and *Uncurable Curses*. You really think your answers are in these?"

"I'm running out of options. These were buried under three inches of dust in the far back corner of my aunt's basement." I shrug. "It's these or nothing."

"You really believe you're incurable?" he asks with a look of disbelief as he opens the first book.

"I hope not, but I've been searching for answers for a long time with no luck in sight." I reach for *The Afterlife UnEarthed* and smirk, knowing exactly how laughable saying I'm looking for luck with a curse like mine sounds.

Caleb slides into the chair near him and stares at me, his

expression captivating and confident. "We are going to find it. I can feel it."

I suck in a breath. *If we both can feel it, does that mean it could happen? It's within reach?*

"What is it? Talk to me." He grabs my hand, and sparks of light rain over the table. I push back, letting go, and watch the embers fade. "You're having an awakening," he says.

My eyes snap back to his. They're full of admiration, sparkling like the lights that just flashed in the room. "How can you be so sure?" I whisper.

"Because I've seen it. Where I'm from there's a witch with shadow magic. Just as rare as light. This happened to her many years ago when I was young."

"You're close with this witch?"

He pauses. "She's my sister."

What? A wizard that is in close contact with not just one but two rare magics possibly. My stomach twists. "How is this possible. If you're right"—he gives me a look like he knows he's right, but I ignore him—"then this would be the first time a shadow and light magic witch were alive in the same time period in over a thousand years. This is impossible."

"Or it's fate," he says matter-of-factly.

I don't want to touch the *fate* idea with a ten-foot pole, so I flip open my book to a random page. "Let's start looking for answers."

Caleb opens his book and scans the table of contents. *Smart.* I check mine to see which section I should start with, but they all look pretty dire. *Stuck in the afterlife. How an earth witch handles death. Life without plants.* I don't think this grimoire is going to help me. I close the book and slide the last one toward me.

The silence in the room is heavy as I open *Uncurable Curses.* I chance using my magic and cast a small spell to the radio behind the counter. Quiet spooky sounds filter through the bookstore's speakers, and I let out a sigh of relief. I want to find answers, but thinking about my curse all day is exhausting.

I wait for the magical backlash, but everything stays still. I scan the curses in my book. *Uncurable warts, uncurable dark magic* (maybe?), *uncurable ailments.* The list goes on and on. I find page 132 for uncurable dark magic.

Fred pops up from the chair near Caleb, making me jump. Caleb scratches him behind the ears, smiling as my crazy cat purrs and soaks up the attention. When Fred's had enough, he walks off to curl up on top of a stack of books.

I bite my lip and return to my page. "We could try this," I say and slide the book to Caleb.

He leans over to read the spell scrawled there, while I glimpse the page he's on in *The Grim Dealings of a Dark Wizard*. He found something on dark wizard curses. Maybe we can try that next.

His finger taps my page, drawing my attention back to him.

I swallow. He's a breath away from the tip of my nose.

"You really want to try this one?" he asks. "Did you read the ingredients?"

"No, I didn't. It just sounded like it could fit." I scan the page and grimace.

A dark wizard needs to be present to cast this spell. As you were cursed by one, so one is needed to be undone.

Well, I don't know any dark wizards, so that isn't going to work. I scan the rest of the ingredients for fun and see it requires blood too. *Ew. No thanks.* I slam my book shut. "I don't think this one is going to work."

Caleb chuckles. "This one seems safe enough." He points to his page, and I scan the list quickly. A handful of herbs I have in the back room, a spell, and I have to lay on a table while Caleb's hands hover over me. Nervous butterflies flutter in the pit of my stomach. Every time we touch, light appears. *What if he is right about fate and we're just playing into her hands?*

I put on my brave face. "Okay, let's do it! Come to the back. I should have everything we need."

He picks up his book and pats a tired Fred before following me to the back. I pull on the third bookshelf from the bottom, and a hidden door swings open. "Wow. That's pretty impressive," he says as he steps across the threshold.

"Witches and books, what can I say? We enjoy our secrets."

I leave him to take in the hundreds of vials neatly lining the shelves on one wall. A large counter with a sink and stove for preparing food sits against the side wall under the shelves, a long table dominates the room's center. "This is where we keep small portions to sell to witches in the community," I explain. Another set of shelves holds spell books and recipes for baking.

"Nice," Caleb says.

I start clearing off the table so I can lay on it for the spell. Then I work on gathering the herbs while Caleb reads them off.

"Bayberries, bay laurel leaves, dried basil, buckeye nuts. Grind all of those together. We need a black candle to carve intentions into while I do the spell," he says.

I scan our small black candle section and grab one big enough to carve into. Then I take a knife from a drawer by the sink and etch into the wax the year I was born along with the curse itself. At the last second, I decide to add *freedom* to it.

I grind the ingredients together. Since I'm the one cursed, it's important for me to do the steps myself. Everything is done with intent. Magic is sensitive. The emotions and energy one puts off while preparing a spell channel into the spell too.

I have to stay focused at all times. Every thought and action should funnel towards being free.

I place the candle and bowl of herbs at the head of the table and lay down. Caleb circles the table and peers into my face. "Are you ready?"

"Let's do it," I say as nervous jitters crawl up my throat.

Chapter Nine

C aleb lights my candle then dips his thumb in oil before dropping it in the herb bowl. He gently smears a line across my forehead and slides my sweater up enough to expose my stomach then repeats the process. I close my eyes and think about the curse being lifted as he starts to recite the spell quietly. I imagine frolicking through the celebration every year, laughing with Becks, and Caleb joining in too.

"Okay, Rachel," Caleb says after a pause. "I'm going to place my palms on your head and stomach and try to push my magic into you. Are you ready?"

I hold all of my hope inside of me and nod.

I let my breaths even out, slow and steady, so I don't hold it all in with anticipation. He places his strong hands first on my head then on my stomach. Heat rushes to the surface in the quiet moment before a light pulse of energy spills from his hands to my skin.

My body spins out of my control. Something surges from my heart outward, making my back arch off the table. My eyes snap open as Caleb disconnects and steps back, looking up. I follow his gaze. Thousands of tiny orbs of light fill the room.

I sit up in amazement. "What—did it work?"

"That wasn't what was supposed to happen, so I'm not sure." His eyes rove over me. "Maybe try using your magic. Earth or light."

I scoff. *There's no way I'm a light wielder.*

I close my eyes. I know what my earth magic thread feels like. After all, I've been using it since I was a child. If there's something else here, I would know. Wouldn't I?

I reach for my earth tether. In my mind's eye I see the deep green thread flowing through my fingers, and then I dig deeper. A soft glow emits farther into my core, but I can't hold onto it. Its essence slips through my mental grasp like fog burning in sunlight.

I sigh. Maybe it wants to stay hidden.

I open my eyes and cast flowers to rain around Caleb. He smiles as rose petals stick to his shirt, but the corners of his mouth drop slightly when they won't come off.

"Okay. I guess we can say it didn't work." He tries to pluck another rosebud off, but it's no use. They are a part of the shirt now. *Oops.*

"That's strange, though," I say.

"What is?"

"Historically, my magic mishaps react only to me. They never target other people." I wave my hand at his now-rose-petalled shirt. "Even in the coffee shop the coffee only spilled on me."

He runs a hand across the back of his neck. "Eh, in the coffee shop I used my magic to avoid the coffee."

"What!" I throw my hands in the air. "You just let hot coffee soak my favorite shirt?"

"Whoa, whoa." Caleb holds his hands up in surrender. "I

didn't know who you were. It was instinct. I'm sorry. But in my defense, I did fix your sweater after."

I draw closer to him, ready to show him where he can shove his instinct, but stop as the magical orbs in the room brighten. "What the—"

Caleb grips my hand before I can step away. "Let me try something."

I make as though to argue, but the words are lost as he draws even closer to me. His entire body presses against mine. I'm sure he knows how fast my heart is beating.

The magical lights flash brighter and blink three times before fading.

I tilt my head to Caleb. "Did you learn what you wanted?"

"I have a hunch. We will find out more soon, I'm sure." He checks his watch. "It's ten already. We aren't going to learn anything from these books. I think it's time we go back to the celebration and see what the spirits have to offer."

I press my hand against his chest. "What if something bad happens?"

Caleb reaches up and takes my hand in his. "I would never let anything bad happen to you, Rachel."

"Okay," I say as Fred tears into the room like his tail is on fire. He flings his body up onto the counter then charges at the glass vials. "Fred, no!"

I reach out with my earth magic and the ground shakes. Fred leaps from the shelves at me, his claws open, ready to snag the first thing he touches, but a *whoosh* of air whips through the room, plucks the cat up, and gently sets him on the ground.

The second Fred is released from the magic, he runs to my legs and tries to climb, but I reach down and scoop him up. His little heart is pitter-pattering at a rapid speed.

"What scared you, bud?" I give Caleb a worried glance before heading back into the main part of the store. I hear

Caleb's footsteps behind me and the click of the secret door latching shut.

I pause, taking in what's in the window as I place a protesting Fred on the ground.

Caleb bumps into my back. "What the—"

Two spirits peer in from the window, their eyes locked on mine. I squint at them, trying to figure out what they want. One of them motions for me to come outside.

"Well, I guess you were right about needing to talk to spirits," I tell Caleb. "But it looks like they found us." I put on my brave girl pants and walk to the door.

"Why can't they come here?"

"The salt," I tell him. "I put it all over this place to keep them away."

Caleb glances around, no doubt spotting the glittering granules covering every seal or crack in the building. "Oh."

My hand grabs the door handle when behind me, Caleb sucks in a breath. "The woman—she looks just like you."

I careen my head in the female ghost's direction. Her lack of color makes it hard to tell if our hair or eye color matches, but her facial structure resembles mine in an eerily similar way. The curve of her eyes, the shape of her nose, and the dimple in her cheek as she smiles unnerve me. She's not identical, but there are freaky similarities.

"Let's see if she knows how to break the curse."

I push open the door and step outside.

Chapter Ten

"Rachel Elara," the female spirit says to me as I pass the threshold.

"Yes, and who are you?"

Her eyes light up as she focuses on the spirit next to her then back to me. "I am Maribel Elara. Your grandmother from centuries ago." She reaches for my hand in her excitement, but it passes through me, leaving a winter chill in its wake.

She frowns. "I'm sorry. I tend to forget on Samhain. I've been looking for you for a long time."

I glance at Caleb. His eyes alight with hope or wonder, I can't be sure which.

"You found me," I say. "What is it you wish to tell me?"

Caleb turns toward me, his eyebrows drawn, but I shake my head. I want to see if my supposed ancestor knows about the curse or if this is all for nothing, as usual.

"We know how to cure it," she says as if reading my mind.

I flinch. "If you know, then why has no one cured it yet?"

Her face falls. "I was the original witch. It's taken centuries for me to become strong enough in the afterlife to approach you. The ones who have come to me before you have told me of their fall." A ghostly tear slides down her cheek. "I never wanted this for my family. I fell in love, you see." She grabs the male ghost next to her. He smiles at her in admiration. "When your soulmate comes into your life, there isn't any other option in the world for you. We were drawn together, and no one could tear us apart. Not even death himself." Maribel studies me then Caleb, her smile stretching.

Oh no. "What about the curse? I'm running out of time before I have to wait another year." *Or worse.*

"Oh my! I'm so sorry. Yes." She looks at us with a glint in her eye. "The curse thrives on the lonely. Your task is to search your heart. *Awaken* your heart."

"But what does that have to do with my parents? The coven always said I needed to understand what happened to them to defeat the curse." I ring my hands together and lick sweat from my lips.

Maribel's face falls. "The coven doesn't know every thing. Your parents . . . didn't have access to the cure. *You do.* They knew the risks. They went to a seer to search for a cure, but they were told about you instead. That you had the ability to break the cycle. The coven doesn't know that every woman in our family after me held the curse. And they all perished. You need to understand that they didn't care about the curse in the end because they had you, and you were all your parents cared about. They went together willingly, knowing you would live a long and full life. The curse is getting stronger through the generations, and everything is happening a lot faster than it did in generations past. In the beginning it feels like a harmless fit of mishaps, but as we ignore it and allow it to fester, it grows. As it latches on and spreads throughout the witch, you will notice markings." I slide my sleeve down, revealing the witch's mark that emerged a few years ago. The coven leaders said it was nothing, even though I remembered tracing a similar one on my mom when I was little. Maribel points to the mark. "It cannot continue to go unchallenged or—"

"Okay. I get it." I yank my sleeve back up covering my shoulder. I don't have time to unpack everything my parents did for me tonight. At least not until I can get rid of this curse. "What do I do?"

"Go where you are strongest and reach deep to awaken your heart." Maribel smiles at me again. "I can see cracks forming already. You're very close, my dear. Your fates are entwined. There is not one without the other." Her hand hovers just over my cheek, as if she's willing herself to solidify once more. Then she and her companion fade away.

Caleb presses closer. "Are you okay? That was a lot of information."

I square my shoulders and shove my feelings down hard. I have a curse to break. I turn toward Caleb, not realizing he's as close as he is. I stumble back when I brush against him, but he reaches out, encircling his arms around me.

"I'm good." I breathe heavily. "We need to get to the forest."

"Of course, earth witch." Caleb smirks then checks his watch. "It's eleven. We only have an hour left."

Ah! How in the Samhain am I going to figure this out in time?

I'm freaking out. My heart bounces in my chest. I feel like I'm going to throw up.

Caleb slips one hand through my fingers, while he places the other on the back of my neck, bringing his forehead to mine. "Breathe, Rachel. Just breathe. In." He sucks in a gulp of air. "And out." He exhales through his mouth. I try to mimic him. "Good. Two more times."

I do as he says, and the more I breathe out, the more my body relaxes. "Thank you."

He wraps both arms around me and cradles my head

against his chest. I hear the slow *thump-thump* of his heart-beat. It's the most calming sound in the world.

"I needed this," I say.

"I know." His voice vibrates against me, sending shivers up my spine.

I hide my smile in his shirt before pulling away. "Okay. Time to go figure this out once and for all."

"Lead the way and I'll follow." He holds out his hand. I take it in mine like it's the most natural thing to do. And we set off together to my favorite spot in the woods.

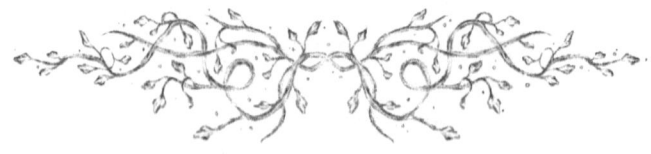

Chapter Eleven

T he path does not have a trail, per se. When I found this spot, I used my earth magic to conjure a small walkway to it that didn't damage the plants, but if a witch didn't know what they were looking for, they wouldn't be able to find it.

I release Caleb's hand. We walk single file, and every few steps, I crouch down to pet the lovely flowers at our feet. "I need to make more time to come out here," I say to myself.

It takes several long minutes to reach our destination. The path isn't a straight line and requires a lot of weaving around natural growths and vegetation. But finally, we make it to a wall of vines, and I look over my shoulder. "Are you ready?" I ask.

Caleb points to the vines. "This is your most powerful spot?"

I throw my head back and laugh, then sweep the vines to one side and duck underneath them. "No, silly. Are you coming?"

"I've done a lot of crazy things in my life, but this is by far the strangest," he mumbles, and I try to hide my giggle. He brushes the vines aside and steps through. "Wow."

His eyes scan over my special place. The forest opens to a wide body of water with a waterfall gently cascading in the back. The landscape beyond the water is mostly flat, decorated with small patches of flowers that I've been tending over the years. Otherwise, it lays open with a lush bed of grass. The trees surrounding the water create a canopy, making this the perfect hideaway. The light rush of the water in the distance is the only sound for miles. "Welcome to my safe haven."

"I don't see why you'd ever leave this place." He whirls around, taking everything in one more time before settling back on me. "Alright. What do we do now?"

I shrug. "I'm not really sure. All she said was, 'Awaken your heart.' She left out the *how*."

"Close your eyes," Caleb says. I'm skeptical as to where this is going, but I'm short on time, so I have to go with it. "Dive deep into your core memories and feelings. Think about all of the times you've felt the most loved."

I picture when I was young and my parents were still alive. They would cuddle me close and smother me with kisses on either side of my face. I loved every second of it. They would do it multiple times a day—it didn't matter if it was a good day or a bad day for them. When it came to me, there was only love.

After they were gone, Aunt Viv stepped into Mom's shoes. She loves baking, so she taught me everything I know. We would stay up late dancing and baking cookies in the kitchen. Singing our hearts out to all of the songs we loved.

Then Becks. She's the sister I never knew I needed. We've done everything together. Gushed over boys, struggled to open our bookstore, and moved in together. But at the end of the day, we cuddle up on our couch with Fred and Klaus, turn on some trashy television, and unbox our day. Eventually, we might have to add on to the house after we each settle down and have our own families, but we love being in each other's space every day. In a word, we're inseparable.

"You're incredible," Caleb whispers.

I open my eyes and the tiny orbs of light are back, reflecting in his eyes as he watches them dance through the air. The warmth surrounding me from thinking of everyone I love gets more intense as I look at Caleb's face. He's staring back at me like he sees forever. A level of admiration I've only ever seen when my dad looked at my mom.

It's hard to explain the cosmic pull of two people. The sparks of fate that ignite like wildfire when two hearts share the same beat.

We walk toward each other until we're nose to nose. "I'm going to kiss you now," I whisper.

His mouth turns up on one side. "It's about time."

I bring my lips to his. The bolt that zapped our fingers earlier in the day is nothing compared to the feelings racing through my body now. Caleb slides his hand through my hair, pulling me closer, deepening our kiss as I'm lost in the bliss of it all. My body hums with energy that radiates off me in waves. This is what using magic feels like but amplified. The area around us warms, a bright light pulsating. I break away and open my eyes with a gasp.

Flowers and greenery of every kind have shot up around us —reds, pinks, yellows, and blues. The orbs of light have split into millions of tiny stars that twirl around us like we've been launched into space. An entire galaxy sits at our fingertips. I reach out to caress a star, and it blends into my skin, becoming part of me. "Wow."

"This is all you," Caleb says in accepted wonder. "The first light witch in centuries." I peer into his eyes, so full of admiration. "*And* an earth witch." He whistles. "That's a lot of power for *my mate*."

"*Fated mates.*" I whisper. My fingers shake as I call the light magic up through my core. It's a shining beacon inside me, something that can't be extinguished now that it's been unleashed. I don't know how it was hidden all this time. But I'm glad it's here now.

I point toward the open canopy above the water, and an arc of sparkling lights shoots from my fingers to the waterfall, illuminating the water and mirroring it back in the reflective surface of the still lake. I laugh. "What else can I do?"

"That's for you to find out, little witch. But I'll be here to cheer you on every step of the way." Caleb pulls me back into his embrace.

"What time is it?" I ask.

I feel him lift an arm behind me. "Eleven fifty-five. So, if your curse was still around, I bet things would have gone a little wild with that display." He chuckles into my hair then places a light kiss on the top of my head. "You're free, little witch."

I scream in my head. *I did it! I finally did it!*

I look to the vines where we came through and see the spirits of my parents, holding each other and smiling at me. I reach my hand out and wave before sending a small sprinkle of light to dance above their heads.

My mom's voice echoes through the grove. "Mates can cure anything." She looks to my dad, "While we weren't mates and the wheels of fate eventually came for us. We had you, and in the end that's all we cared about. Loving you and each other. Be free my sweet daughter." They fade from sight.

A lightness fills me from within. I send another burst of stars above Caleb.

He smirks. "Show off."

"You like it," he lifts me off the ground, so we're nose to nose. "You're stuck with me."

Caleb hums. "No. We're mated. Which is so much better."

A Note to You

Thank you for reading my romances! I appreciate each and every one of you for taking a chance on my stories. I have so many more to show you, and I can't wait to share them.

About the Author

K.P. Knupp received her Master of Science in Biology, specializing in microbiology, ecology, aquatic, and marine from the University of Houston–Clear Lake, she's currently living in Minnesota. In between work and spending time with her husband, son, and her wild German Shepherd, Nyx, she enjoys reading and writing. If there's time to spare, she enjoys creating stickers and mugs!

    Contact K.P.Knupp
    Instagram/Threads/TikTok: @KPKnupp
    Website: kpknupp.com
    Goodreads.com/kpknupp

Also by K.P. Knupp

<u>Snowed In at the Cabin</u>

Alexandra (Alex) Lewis has been biding her time—putting in late nights and early mornings—to become the web designer at Johnson Enterprise. After being passed over (again and again) she makes the rash decision to quit her job. She now has limited time to find a new career or risk having to move back in with her parents.

Desperate to make a living on her art, she needs to find a way back to her creativity and build up her portfolio. Alex impulsively books a secluded getaway at a cabin in the woods. When a wild winter storm comes crashing through faster than initially anticipated, she ends up snowed in with the owner of the cabin, James Edward. The same James who she can't seem to stop bumping into after quitting her job. He seems to be everywhere. From moving into the same building to faking a relationship when her newly ex-boyfriend shows up at the club, they're drawn together.

Snowed in at a cabin in the woods seems fine until the power goes out, and they're left with one bed in front of the fireplace to stay warm. Will the bubble break once they're free from the cabin?

<u>The Witch's Curse</u>

Rachel's curse is nothing new. She's dealt with it her entire life. One day every year filled with bad luck.

But when Caleb, a handsome wizard ,comes to town, things start getting worse than ever before. Spilled coffee is one thing. But when her magic starts backfiring and a seers premonition looms overhead, it's time to dig deeper for a cure.

Rachel and Caleb have one day to unravel the curse, or risk it becoming worse than they could ever imagine.

A Wild Run

We put together this anthology to showcase the very real enigma of human creation. In a world increasingly complacent with AI, we wanted to prove a point: You can give the same prompt over and over to a machine and it will spit out the same, if not largely similar output. Give authors the same prompt... and watch what the human mind can do.

This Mess We Live In

Through the various degrees of life we experience love and pain. To be able to experience it at all is a blessing, but at times it still hurts. While new love can light you up again.

This is for the healing journey. For the fear of the unknown and how diving in can often times be the only answer.

There's brightness on the other side, you just have to keep going.

Fade

Ali doesn't know if she's going crazy, or if what she's feeling is real. There's a presence trying to get her attention, but what happens when she decides to believe.